CONTENTS

His name is Captain America's Wonder Shorts.

ROCKFORD PUBLIC LIBRARY

SPIDER-MAN: WEB DESIGNERS

CREDITS

LETTERER
VC's JOE CARAMAGNA

ON THE COVER
SPIDER-TIME OF NIGHT!
By JACOB CHABOT

ASSISTANT EDITOR
DANNY KHAZEM

EDITOR
DEVIN LEWIS

CONSULTING EDITOR
SANA AMANAT

EXECUTIVE EDITOR
NICK LOWE

EDITOR IN CHIEF
C.B. CEBULSKI

PRESIDENT
DAN BUCKLEY

CHIEF CREATIVE OFFICER
JOE QUESADA

EXECUTIVE PRODUCER
ALAN FINE

SPIDER-MAN CREATED BY STAN LEE & STEVE DITKO

Spotlight

ABDOBOOKS.COM

Reinforced library bound edition published in 2020 by Spotlight,
a division of ABDO, PO Box 398166, Minneapolis, Minnesota 55439.
Spotlight produces high-quality reinforced library bound editions for
schools and libraries. Published by agreement with Marvel Characters, Inc.

Printed in the United States of America, North Mankato, Minnesota.
092019
012020

marvelkids.com
© 2020 MARVEL

Library of Congress Control Number: 2019942395

Publisher's Cataloging-in-Publication Data

Names: Fisch, Sholly; Templeton, Ty, authors. | Del Pennino, Mario; Campbell, Jim;
    Smith, Kieren, illustrators.
Title: Spider-Man: web designers / by Sholly Fisch, and Ty Templeton; illustrated by
    Mario Del Pennino, Jim Campbell, and Kieren Smith.
Description: Minneapolis, Minnesota : Spotlight, 2020. | Series: Marvel super hero
    adventures graphic novels
Summary: Spider-Man and his web-slinging friends are back in this action-packed
    tale of adventure.
Identifiers: ISBN 9781532144554 (lib. bdg.)
Subjects: LCSH: Spider-Man (Fictitious character)--Juvenile fiction. | Parker, Peter
    Benjamin (Fictitious character)--Juvenile fiction. | Superheroes--Juvenile fiction.
    | Good and evil--Juvenile fiction. | Adventure stories--Juvenile fiction. | Graphic
    novels--Juvenile fiction. | Comic books, strips, etc.--Juvenile fiction.
Classification: DDC 741.5--dc23

Spotlight

A Division of ABDO
abdobooks.com

Kid Pick!

Title: _____

Author: _____

Picked by: _____

_____

Why I love this book:

_____
_____
_____
_____
_____
_____
_____
_____

Please return this form to
Mrs Heather in Youth Services or email
your review to
hgunnell@rockfordpubliclibrary.org

 ROCKFORD PUBLIC LIBRARY

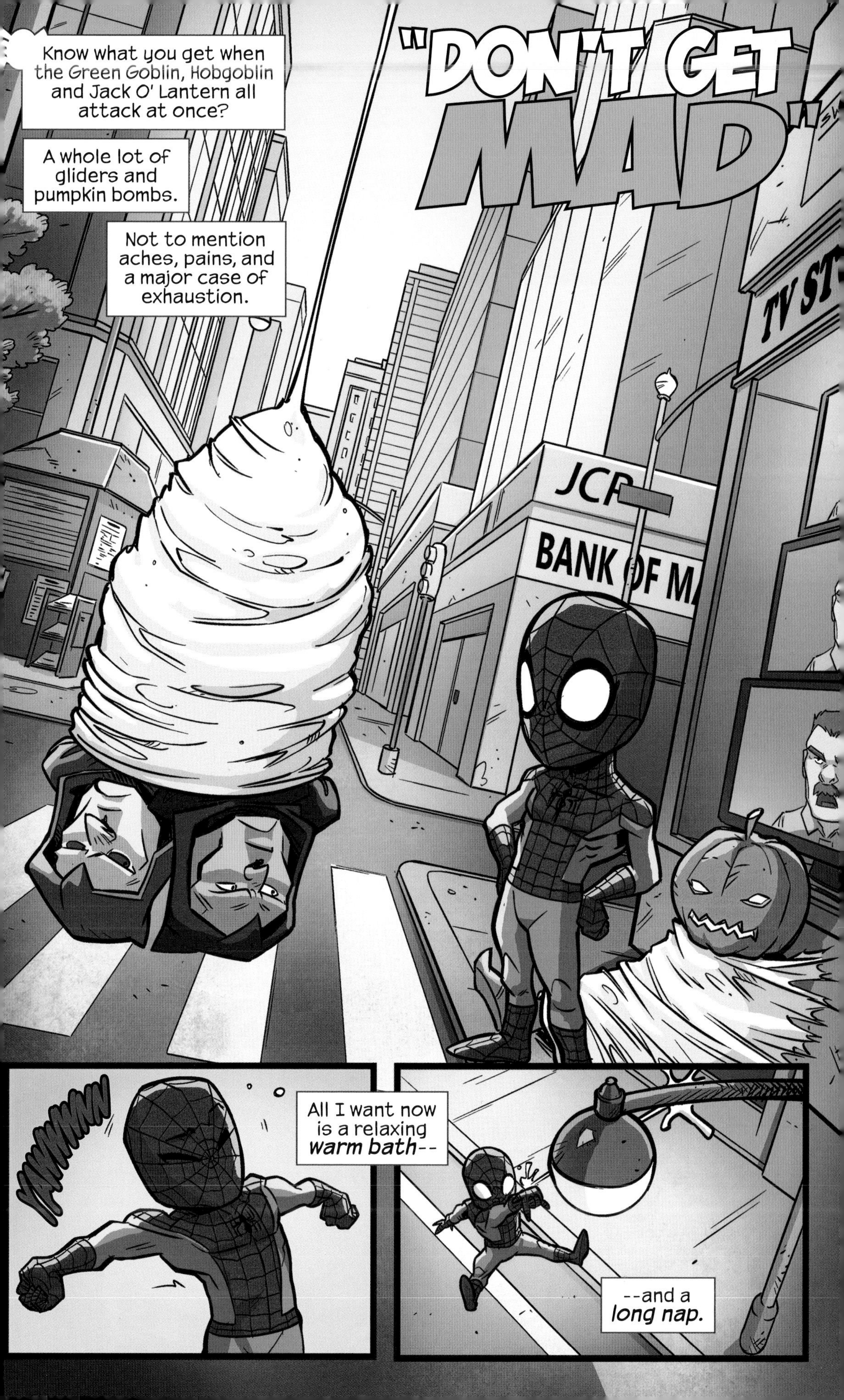
Know what you get when the Green Goblin, Hobgoblin and Jack O' Lantern all attack at once?
"DON'T GET MAD"
A whole lot of gliders and pumpkin bombs.
Not to mention aches, pains, and a major case of exhaustion.
JCP
BANK OF M
TV ST
YAWWWNN
All I want now is a relaxing *warm bath*--
--and a *long nap.*

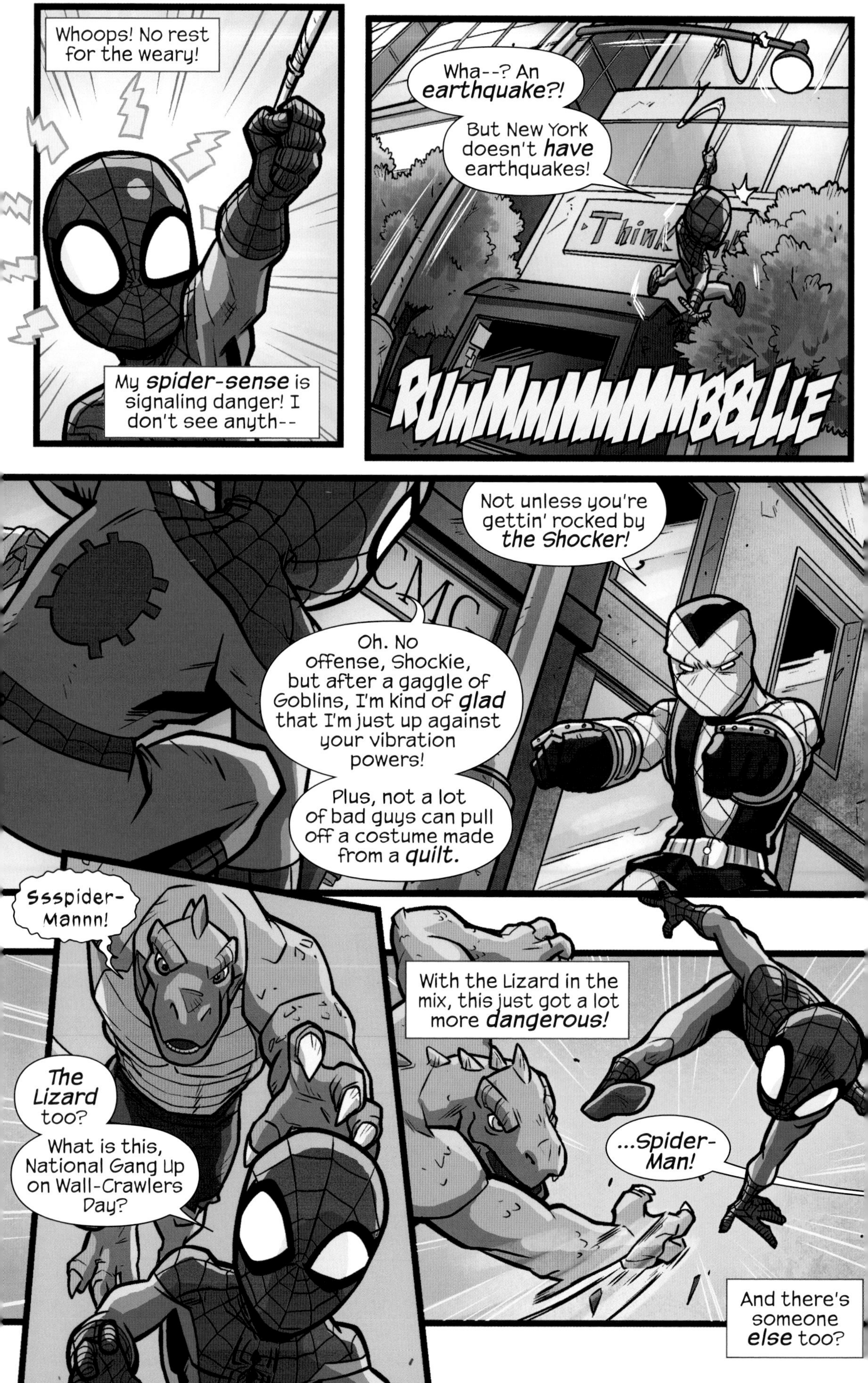

Whoops! No rest for the weary!
My spider-sense is signaling danger! I don't see anyth--
Wha--? An earthquake?!
But New York doesn't have earthquakes!
RUMMMMMMMMBBLLE
Not unless you're gettin' rocked by the Shocker!
Oh. No offense, Shockie, but after a gaggle of Goblins, I'm kind of glad that I'm just up against your vibration powers!
Plus, not a lot of bad guys can pull off a costume made from a quilt.
Ssspider-Mannn!
The Lizard too?
What is this, National Gang Up on Wall-Crawlers Day?
With the Lizard in the mix, this just got a lot more dangerous!
...Spider-Man!
And there's someone else too?

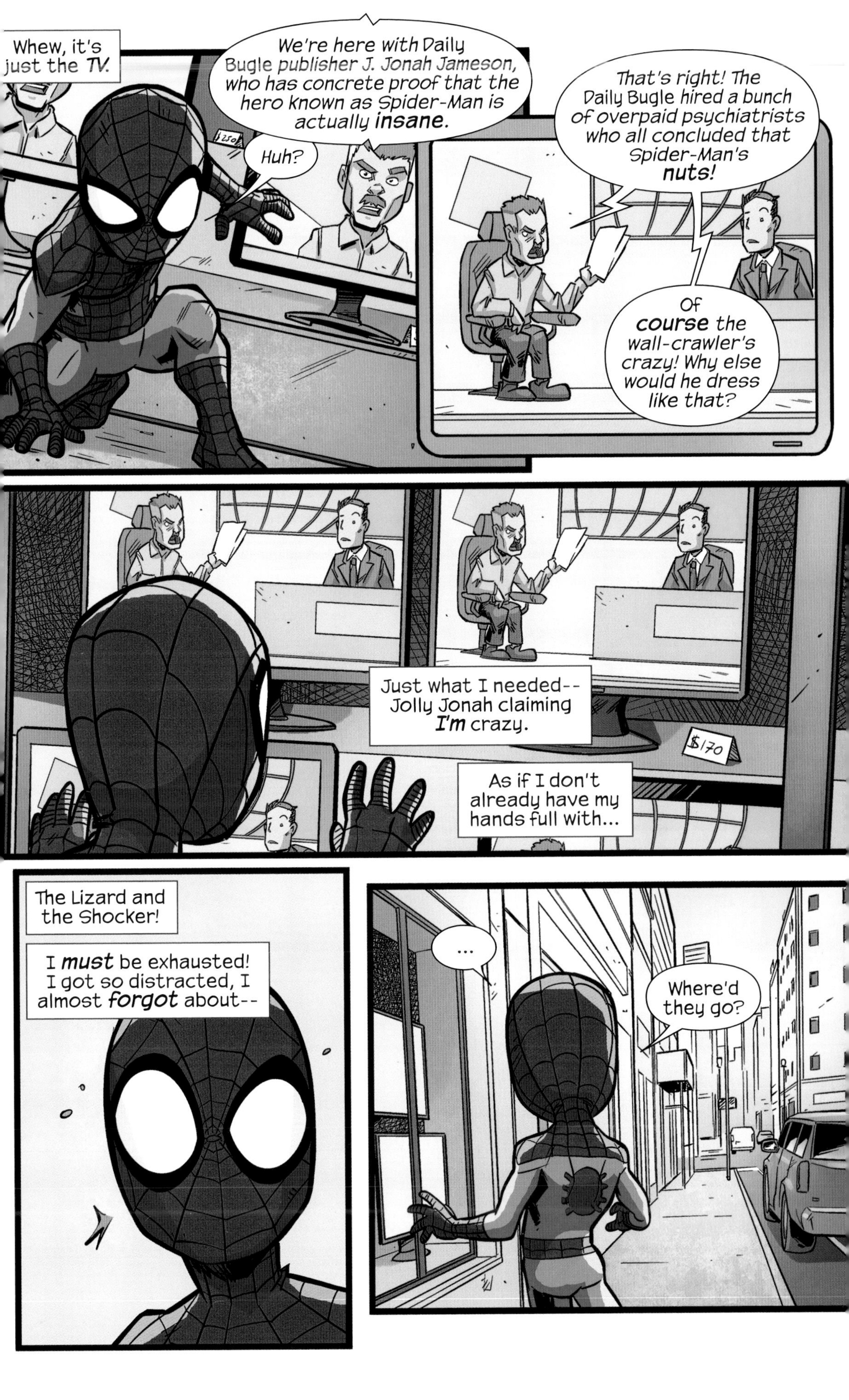
Whew, it's just the TV.
We're here with Daily Bugle publisher J. Jonah Jameson, who has concrete proof that the hero known as Spider-Man is actually insane.
Huh?
That's right! The Daily Bugle hired a bunch of overpaid psychiatrists who all concluded that Spider-Man's nuts!
Of course the wall-crawler's crazy! Why else would he dress like that?
Just what I needed-- Jolly Jonah claiming I'm crazy.
$170
As if I don't already have my hands full with...
The Lizard and the Shocker!
I must be exhausted! I got so distracted, I almost forgot about--
...
Where'd they go?

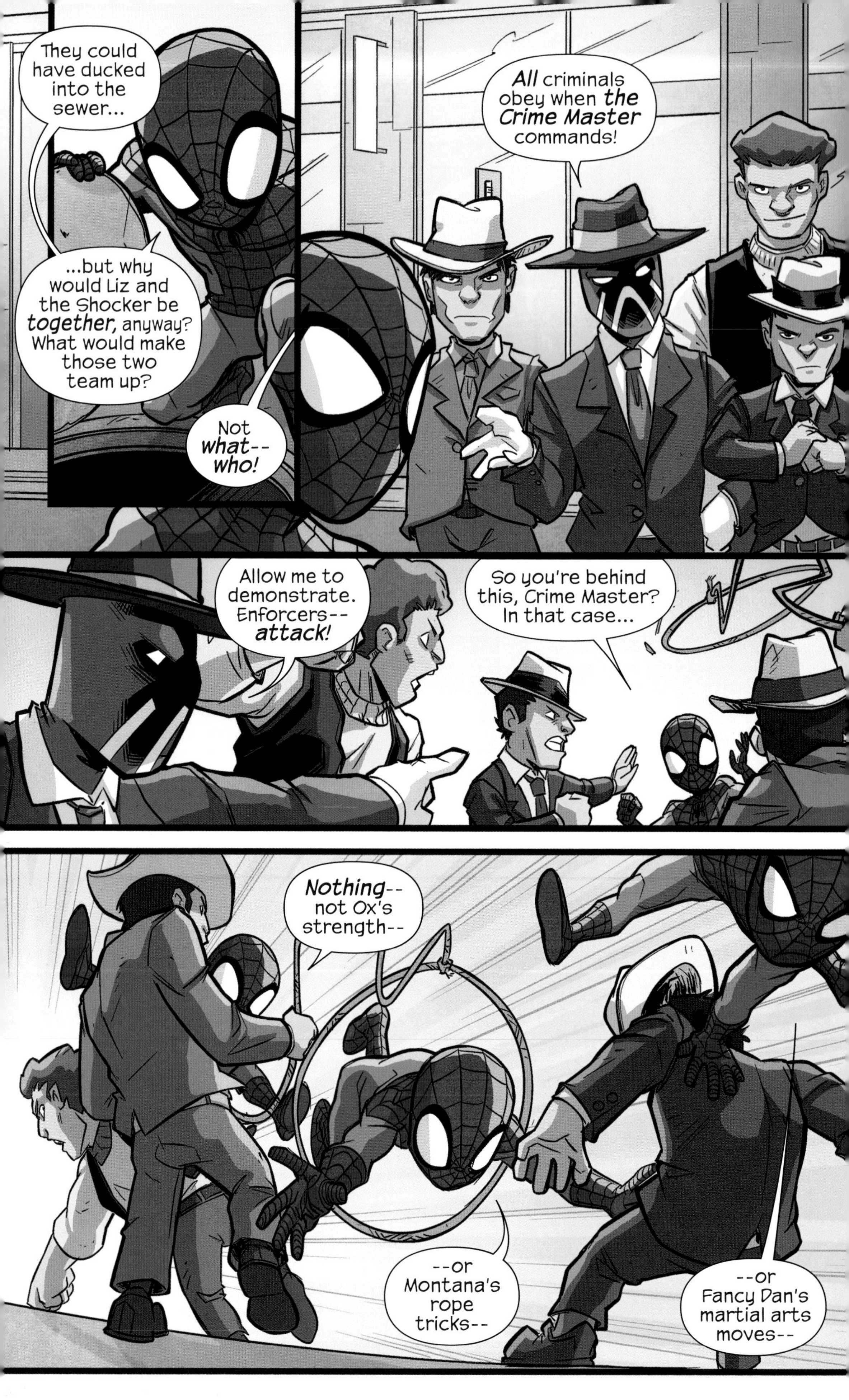
They could have ducked into the sewer...
...but why would Liz and the Shocker be together, anyway? What would make those two team up?
Not what--who!
All criminals obey when the Crime Master commands!
Allow me to demonstrate. Enforcers--attack!
So you're behind this, Crime Master? In that case...
Nothing--not Ox's strength--
--or Montana's rope tricks--
--or Fancy Dan's martial arts moves--

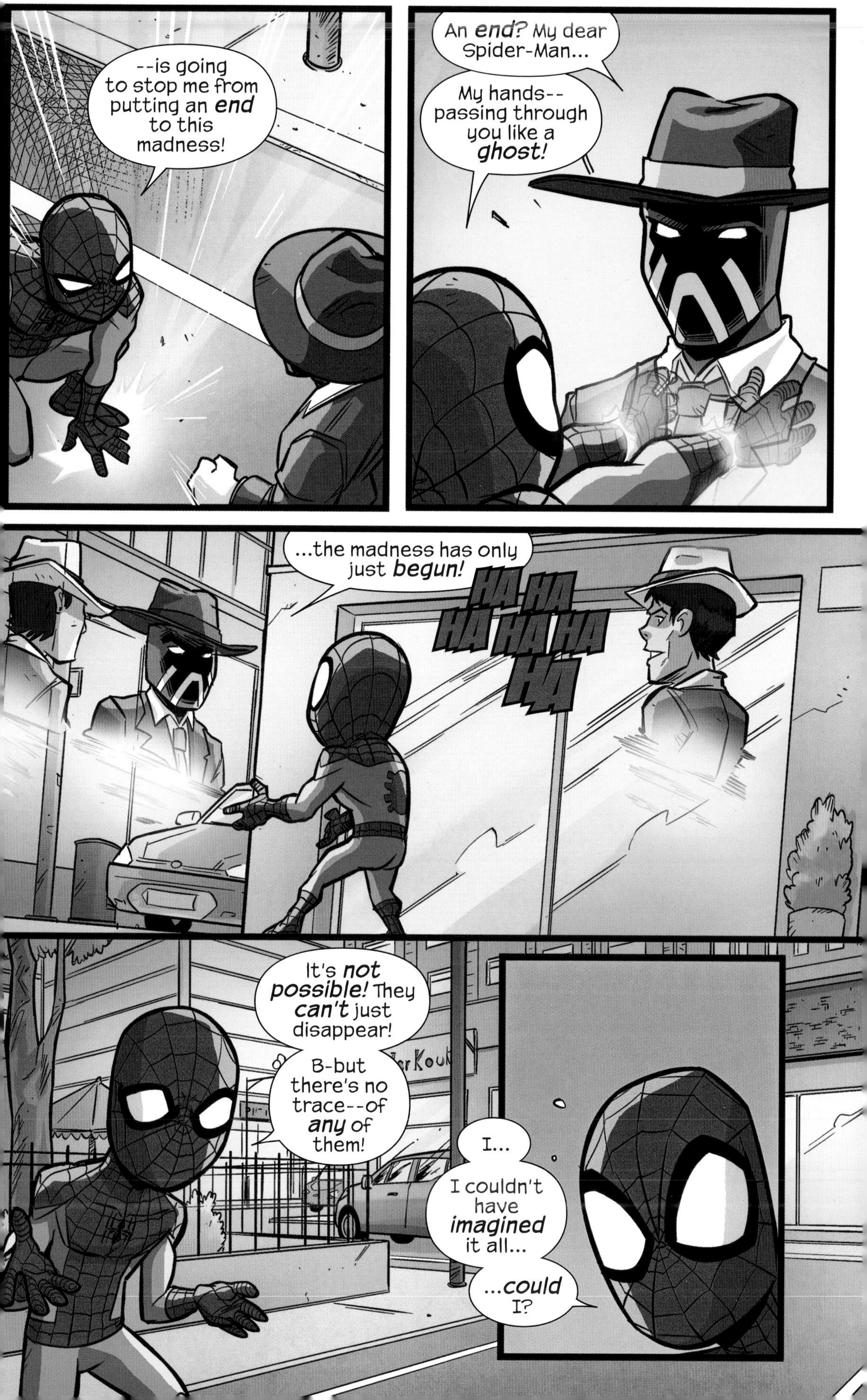
--is going to stop me from putting an end to this madness!
An end? My dear Spider-Man...
My hands--passing through you like a ghost!
...the madness has only just begun!
HA HA HA HA HA HA
It's not possible! They can't just disappear!
B-but there's no trace--of any of them!
I...
I couldn't have imagined it all...
...could I?

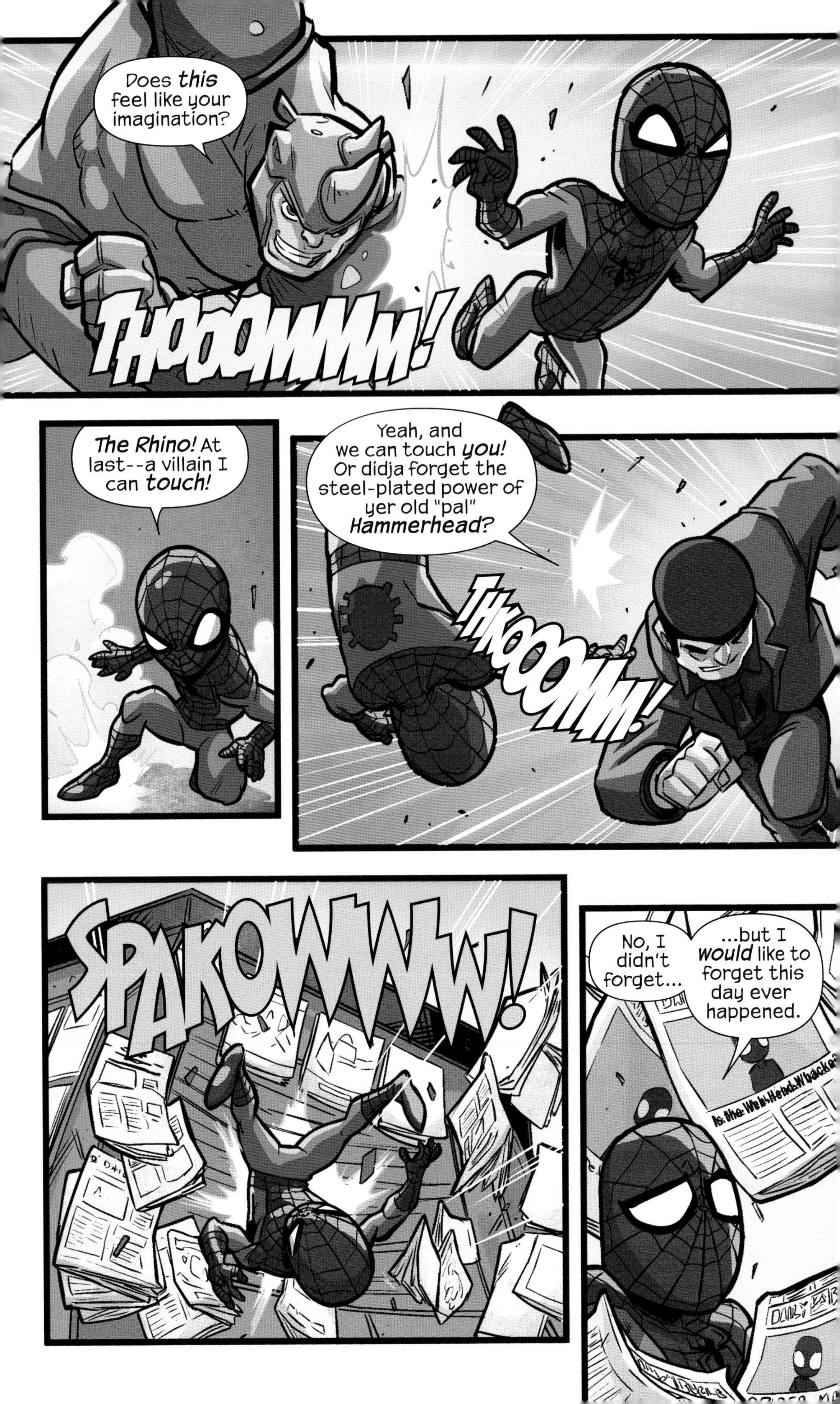
Does *this* feel like your imagination?
THOOOMMMM!
The Rhino! At last--a villain I can *touch!*
Yeah, and we can touch *you!* Or didja forget the steel-plated power of yer old "pal" *Hammerhead?*
THOOOOMM!
SPAKOWWWW!
No, I didn't forget...
...but I *would* like to forget this day ever happened.
Is the Web-Head Whacked

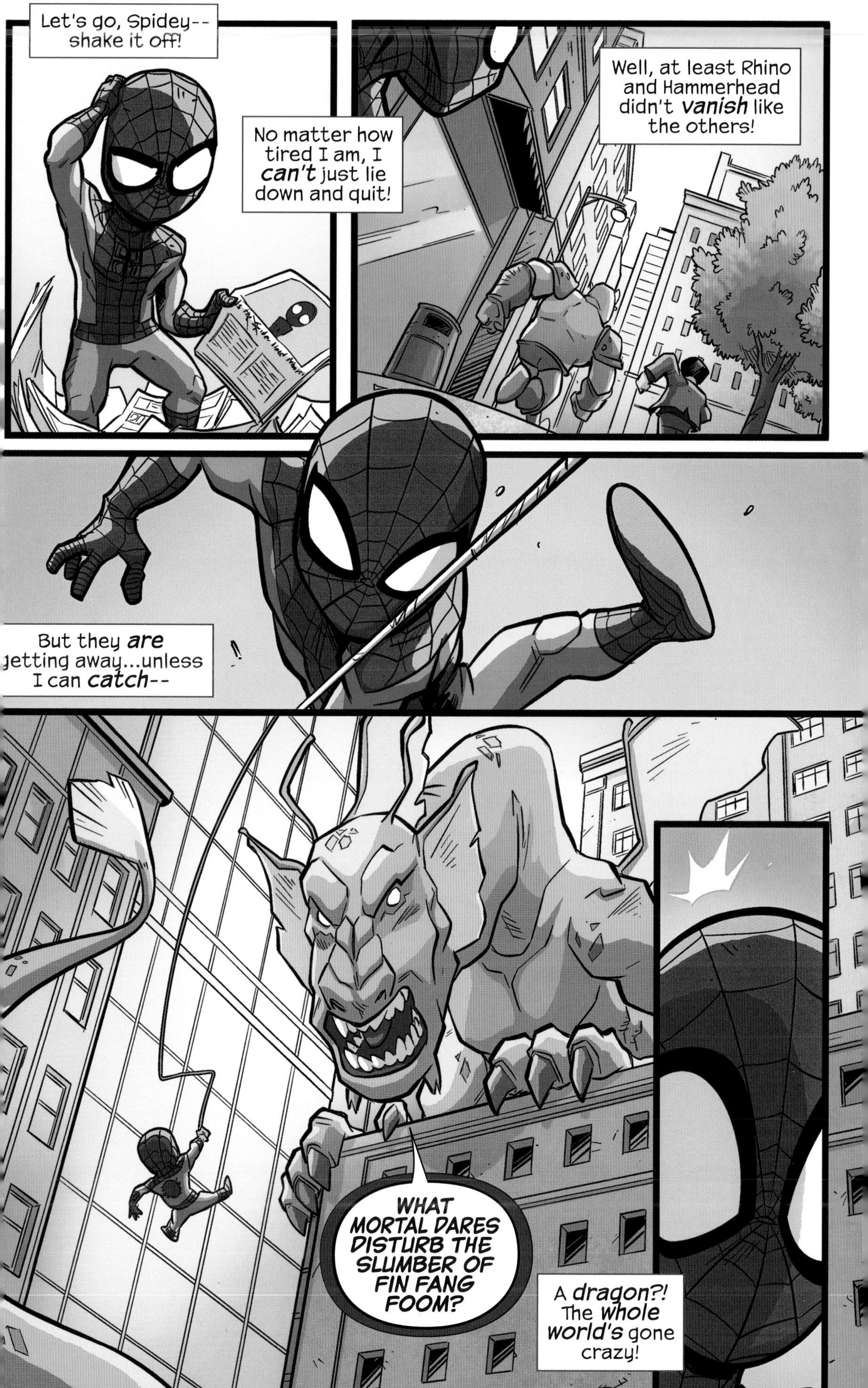
Let's go, Spidey--
shake it off!
No matter how tired I am, I *can't* just lie down and quit!
Well, at least Rhino and Hammerhead didn't *vanish* like the others!
But they *are* getting away...unless I can *catch*--
WHAT MORTAL DARES DISTURB THE SLUMBER OF FIN FANG FOOM?
A *dragon?!* The *whole world's* gone crazy!

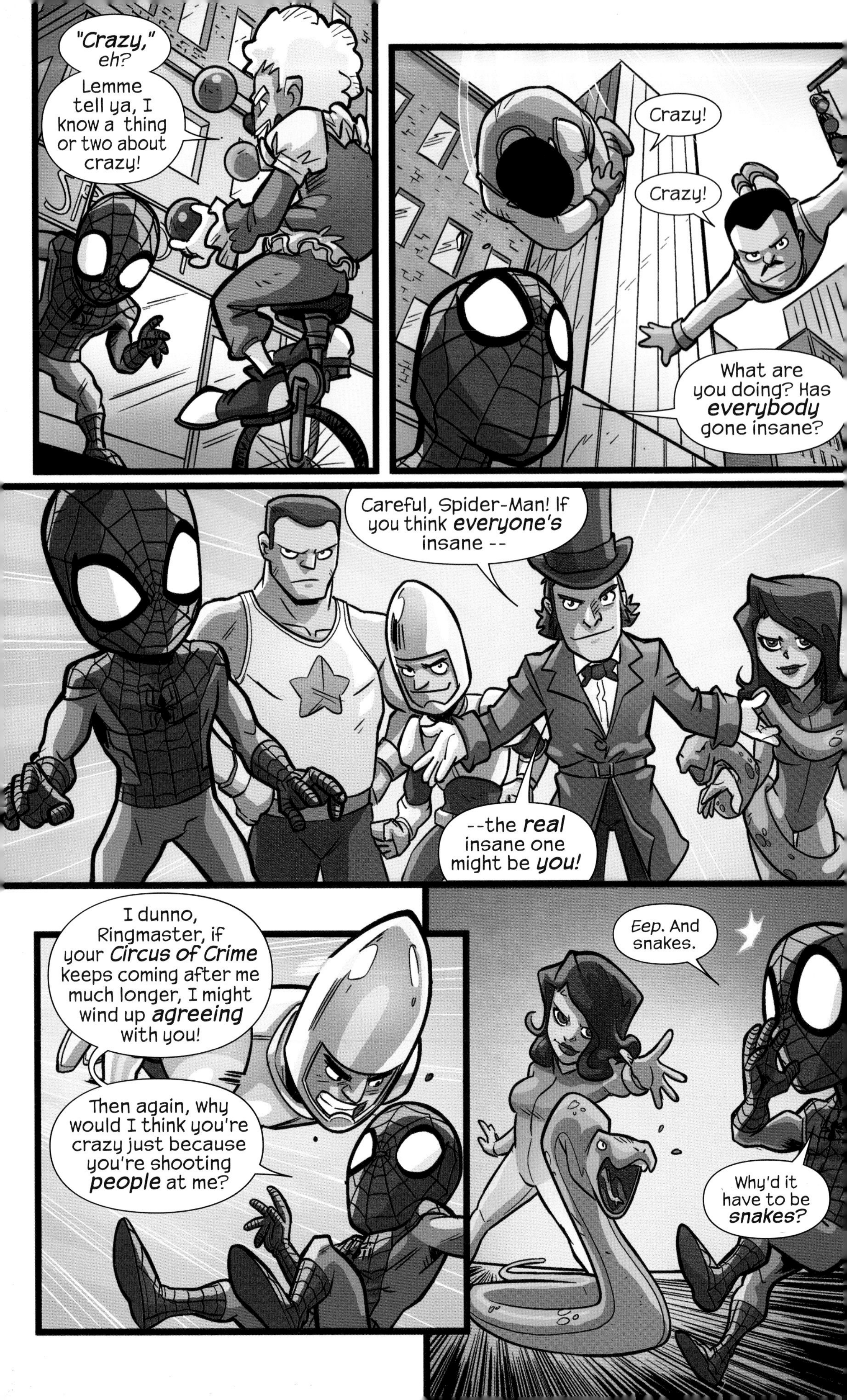

"Crazy," eh? Lemme tell ya, I know a thing or two about crazy!
Crazy!
Crazy!
What are you doing? Has everybody gone insane?
Careful, Spider-Man! If you think everyone's insane --
--the real insane one might be you!
I dunno, Ringmaster, if your Circus of Crime keeps coming after me much longer, I might wind up agreeing with you!
Then again, why would I think you're crazy just because you're shooting people at me?
Eep. And snakes.
Why'd it have to be snakes?

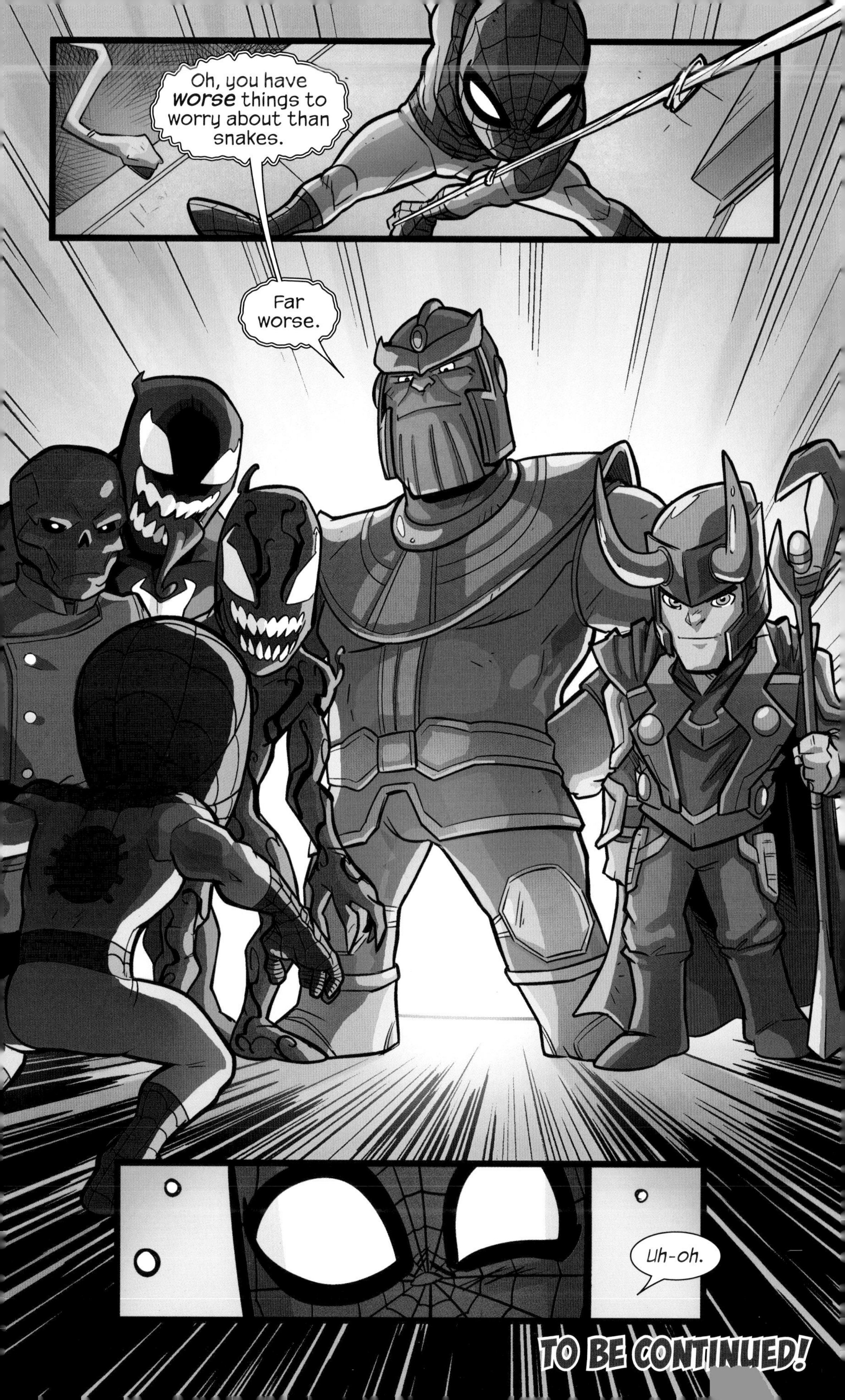
Oh, you have *worse* things to worry about than snakes.
Far worse.
Uh-oh.
TO BE CONTINUED!

"COBWEBS"
featuring your
Friendly Neighborhood
Spider-Man
WHAT ARE YOU DOING ON THE TOOL-SHED?
WRITING A NOVEL.
It was a dank and steamy night. Suddenly, a scream rang out...
"What is it, my love?" he said. "I think I saw a cockroach over there," she said.
"I'll get it with my shoe," he said. "Oh, my brave, strong man!" she said.
"It's not a cockroach after all, my love," he said. "It's a spider..."
He raised his shoe to smash the little creature when, suddenly, he was hit by lightning coming through the window.
It burnt his hair, making him ugly and funny-smelling, so she left him.
The End.
PEOPLE WHO HURT SPIDERS DON'T DESERVE LOVE.

PunchDude
PURPLEPANTS
GRR!
HULK SMASH OCTOPUS-MAN!
NOT ME, YOU IDIOT, I'M THE REFEREE!
REMEMBER, YOU AGREED TO THIS PRIZE FIGHT BECAUSE THE WINNER GETS 100 CLAMS!
HULK HATES CLAMS.
YES, BUT WITH A HUNDRED OF 'EM, YOU CAN TAKE SQUIRREL GIRL TO THE MOVIES ON FRIDAY.
HI.
HULK LIKES NICE SQUIRREL LADY.
STOP THINKING HAPPY THOUGHTS. WE NEED YOU MEAN AND GREEN TO DEFEAT YOUR OPPONENT!
LADIES AND GENTLE-MEN... NOW ENTERING THE RING...
...NA-MOR-MAID-MAN! KING OF THE SEVEN SEAS!
YAY!
HULK'S FAVORITE HERO, SINCE HULK WAS A BOY!
HULK NEVER BEEN SO...
...HAPPY!
WAIT, WHAT AM I DOING UNDERWATER?

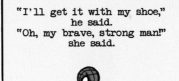

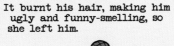

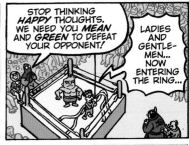

script and art: Ty Templeton

colors: Keiren Smith

Peter and Miles's New Super Hero

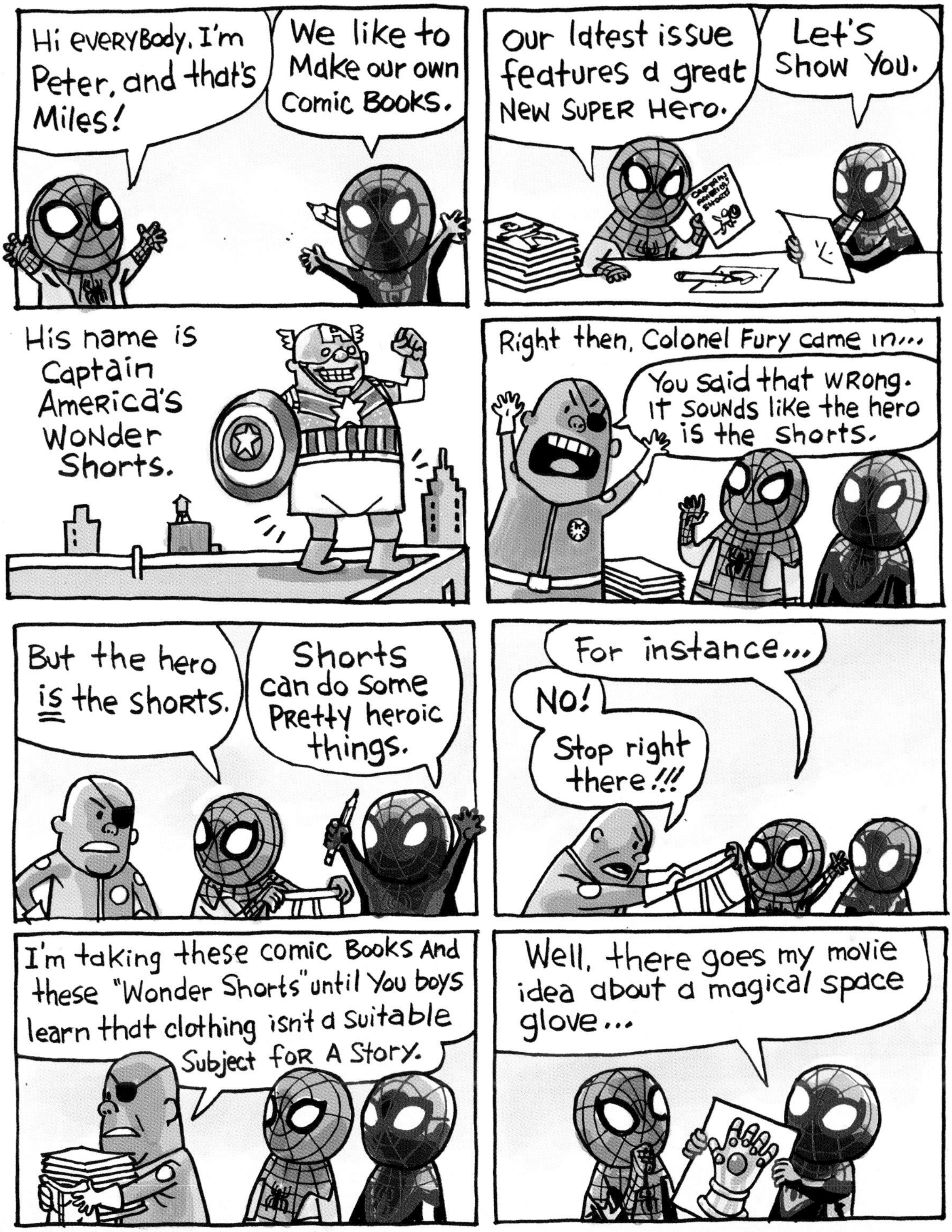
Hi everybody. I'm Peter, and that's Miles!
We like to make our own comic books.
Our latest issue features a great new super hero.
Let's show you.
His name is Captain America's Wonder Shorts.
Right then, Colonel Fury came in...
You said that wrong. It sounds like the hero is the shorts.
But the hero is the shorts.
Shorts can do some pretty heroic things.
For instance...
No!
Stop right there!!!
I'm taking these comic books and these "Wonder Shorts" until you boys learn that clothing isn't a suitable subject for a story.
Well, there goes my movie idea about a magical space glove...

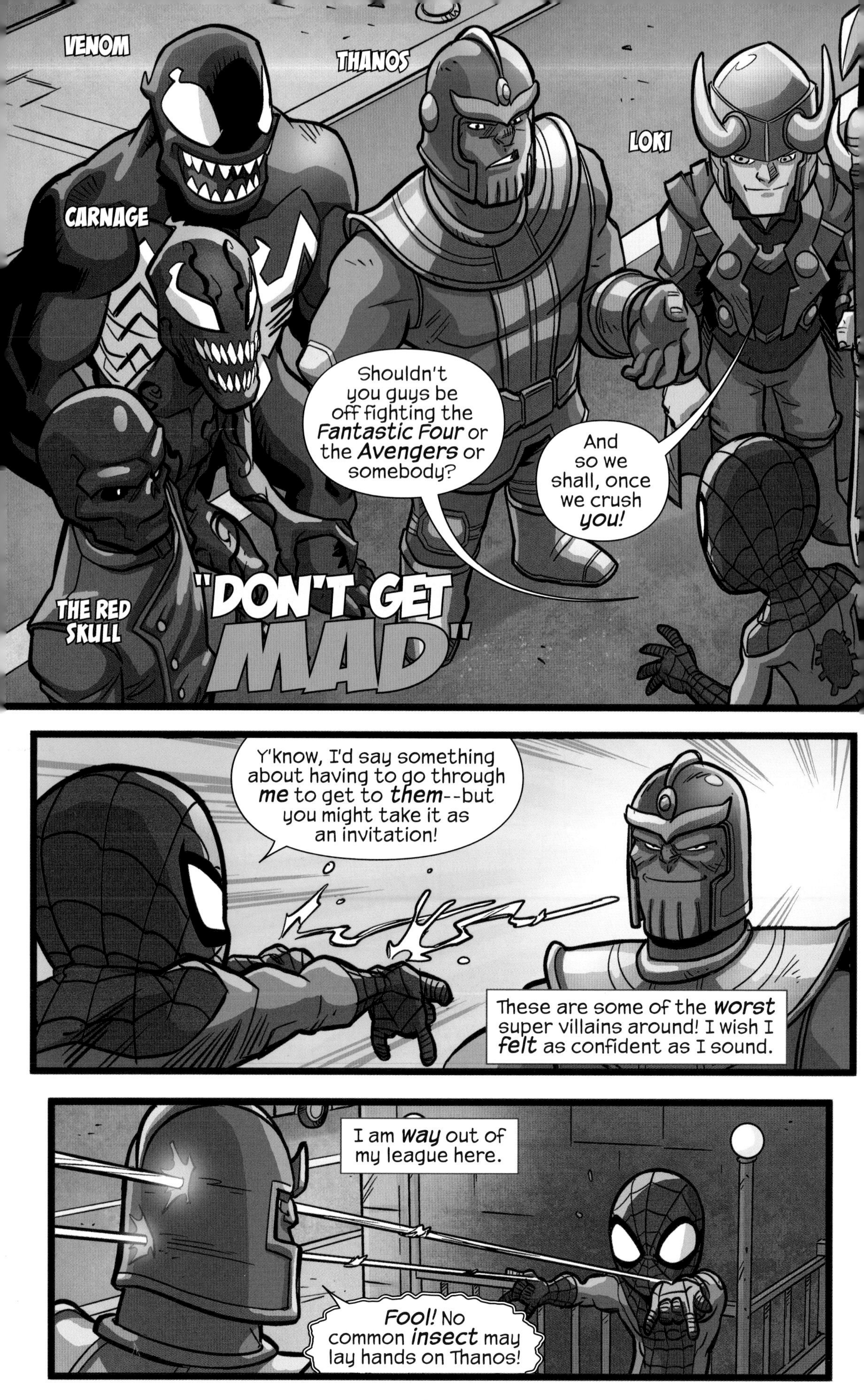

VENOM
THANOS
LOKI
CARNAGE
THE RED SKULL
"DON'T GET MAD"
Shouldn't you guys be off fighting the *Fantastic Four* or the *Avengers* or somebody?
And so we shall, once we crush *you!*
Y'know, I'd say something about having to go through *me* to get to *them*--but you might take it as an invitation!
These are some of the *worst* super villains around! I wish I *felt* as confident as I sound.
I am *way* out of my league here.
Fool! No common *insect* may lay hands on Thanos!

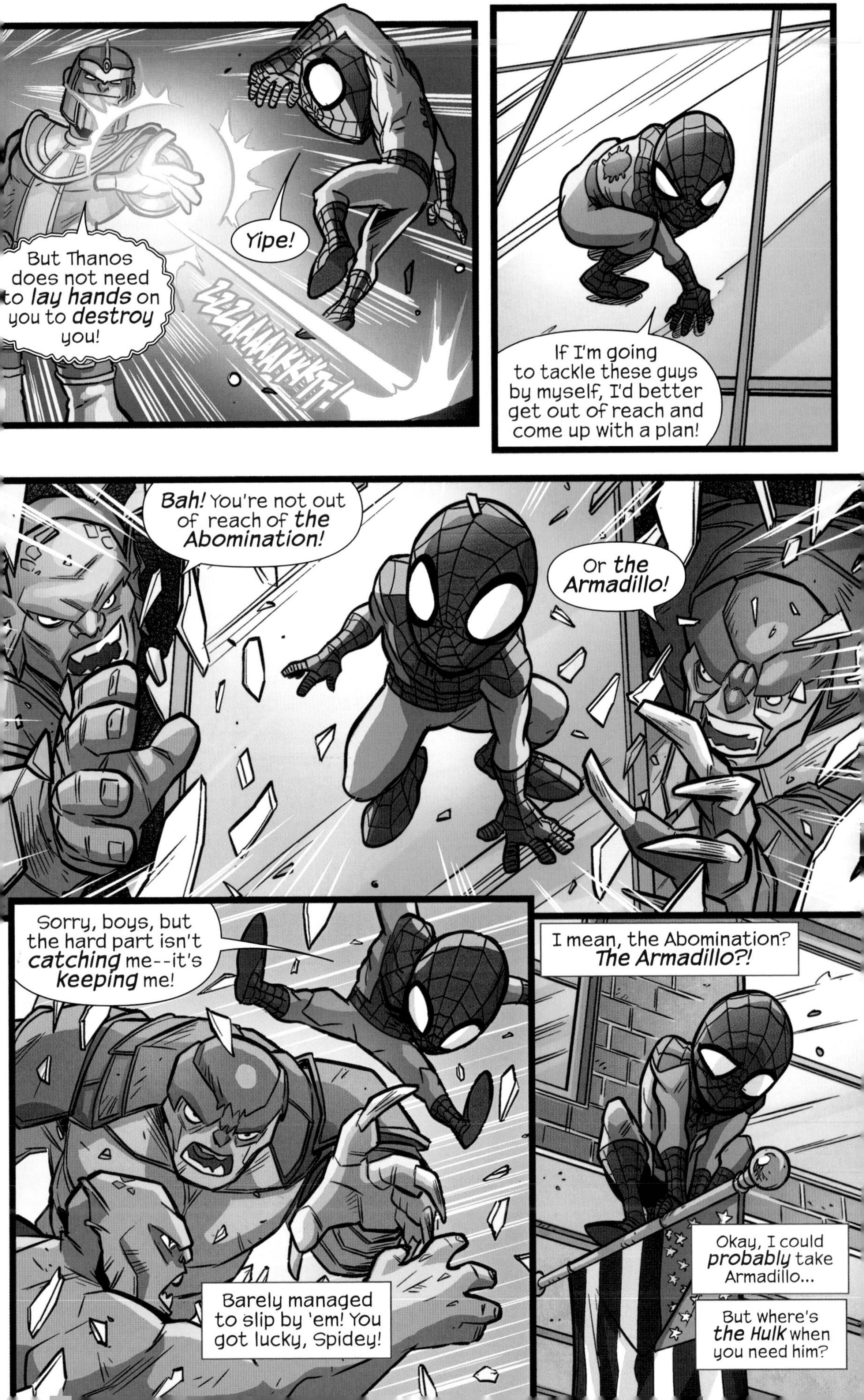
But Thanos does not need to *lay hands* on you to *destroy* you!
Yipe!
ZZZAAAAKKKT!
If I'm going to tackle these guys by myself, I'd better get out of reach and come up with a plan!
Bah! You're not out of reach of *the Abomination!*
Or *the Armadillo!*
Sorry, boys, but the hard part isn't *catching* me--it's *keeping* me!
Barely managed to slip by 'em! You got lucky, Spidey!
I mean, the Abomination? *The Armadillo?!*
Okay, I could *probably* take Armadillo...
But where's *the Hulk* when you need him?

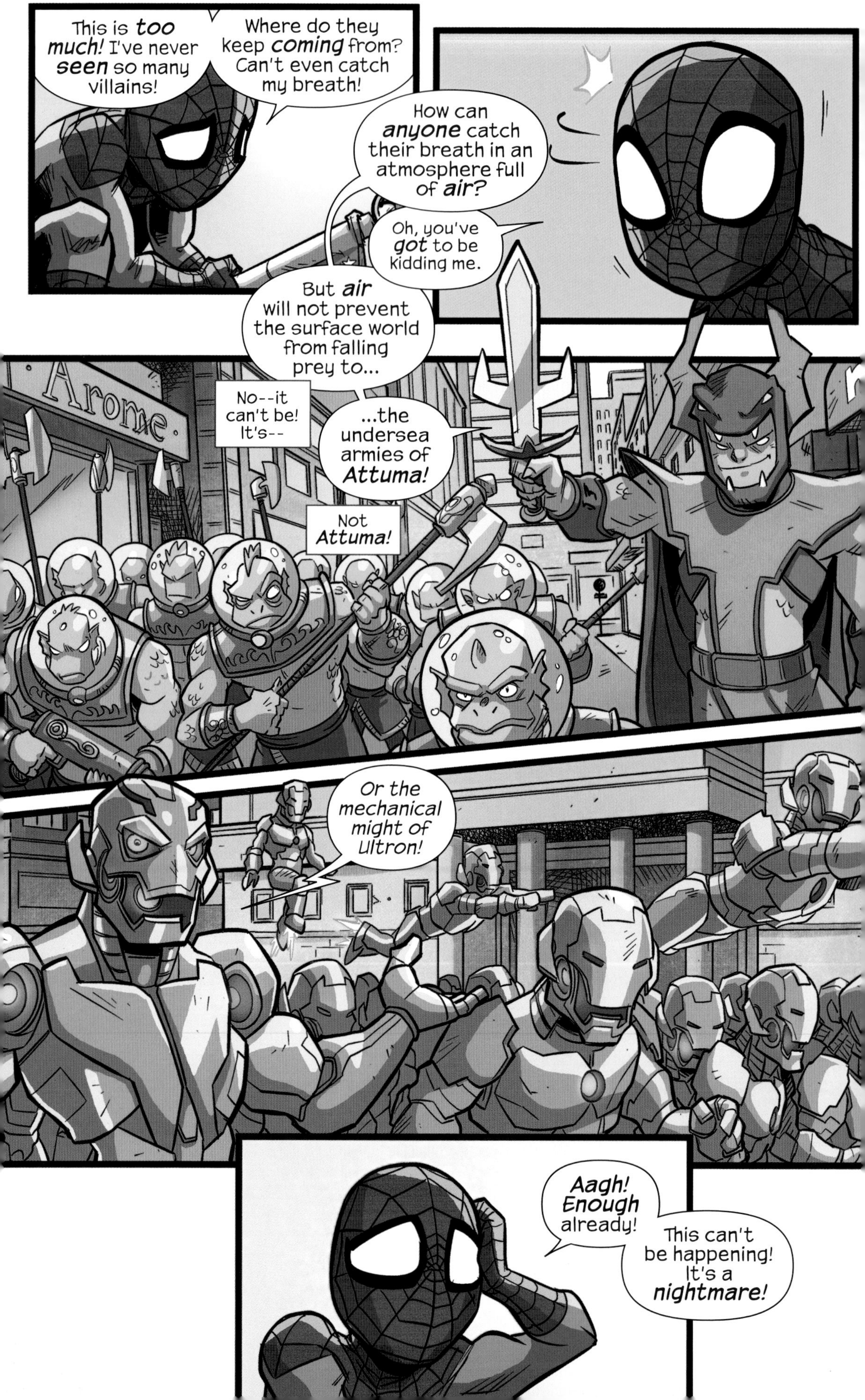
This is too much! I've never seen so many villains!
Where do they keep coming from? Can't even catch my breath!
How can anyone catch their breath in an atmosphere full of air?
Oh, you've got to be kidding me.
But air will not prevent the surface world from falling prey to...
No--it can't be! It's--
...the undersea armies of Attuma!
Not Attuma!
Arome
Or the mechanical might of Ultron!
Aagh! Enough already!
This can't be happening! It's a nightmare!

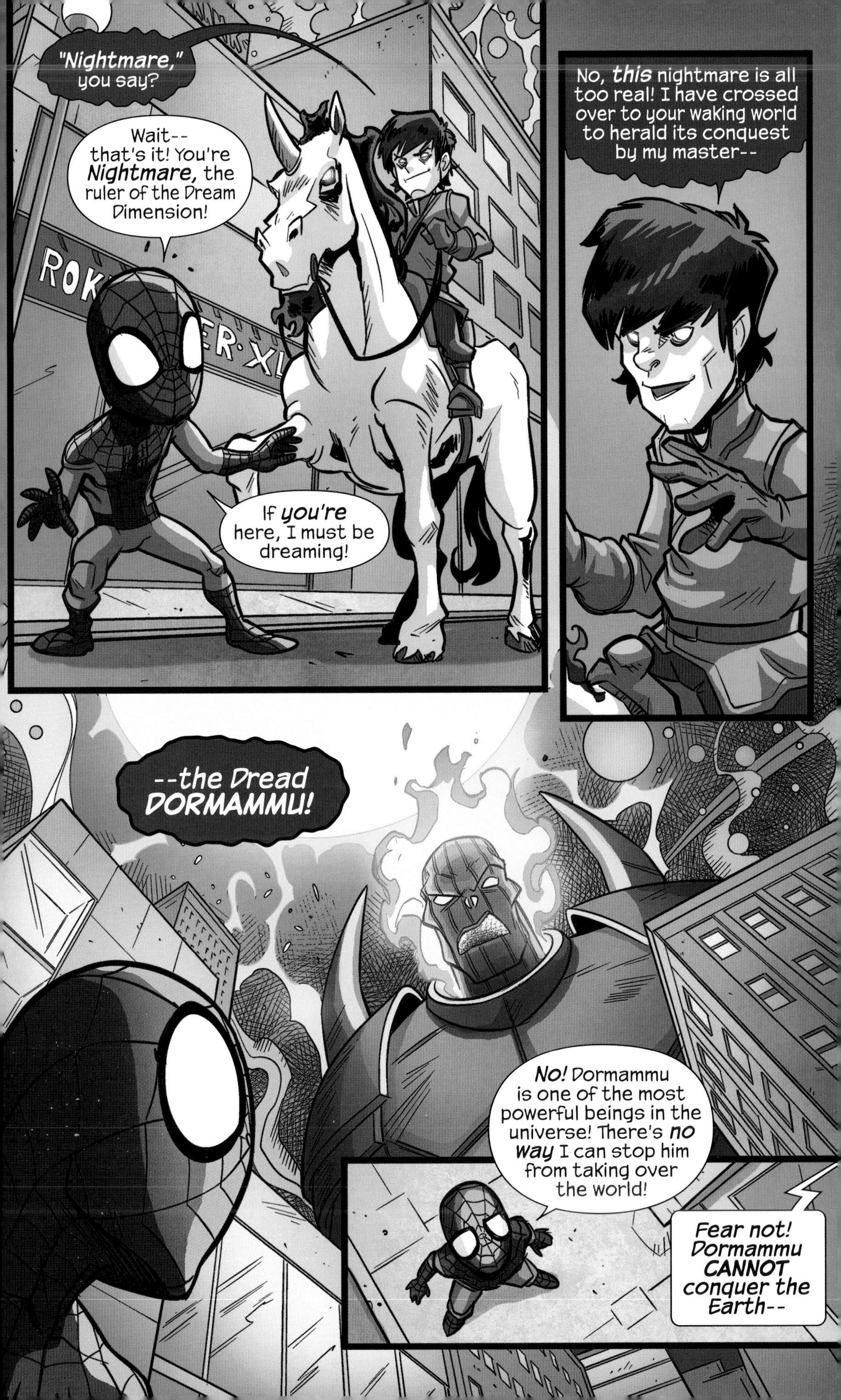
"Nightmare," you say?
Wait-- that's it! You're Nightmare, the ruler of the Dream Dimension!
ROK
ER·XL
If you're here, I must be dreaming!
No, this nightmare is all too real! I have crossed over to your waking world to herald its conquest by my master--
--the Dread DORMAMMU!
No! Dormammu is one of the most powerful beings in the universe! There's no way I can stop him from taking over the world!
Fear not! Dormammu CANNOT conquer the Earth--

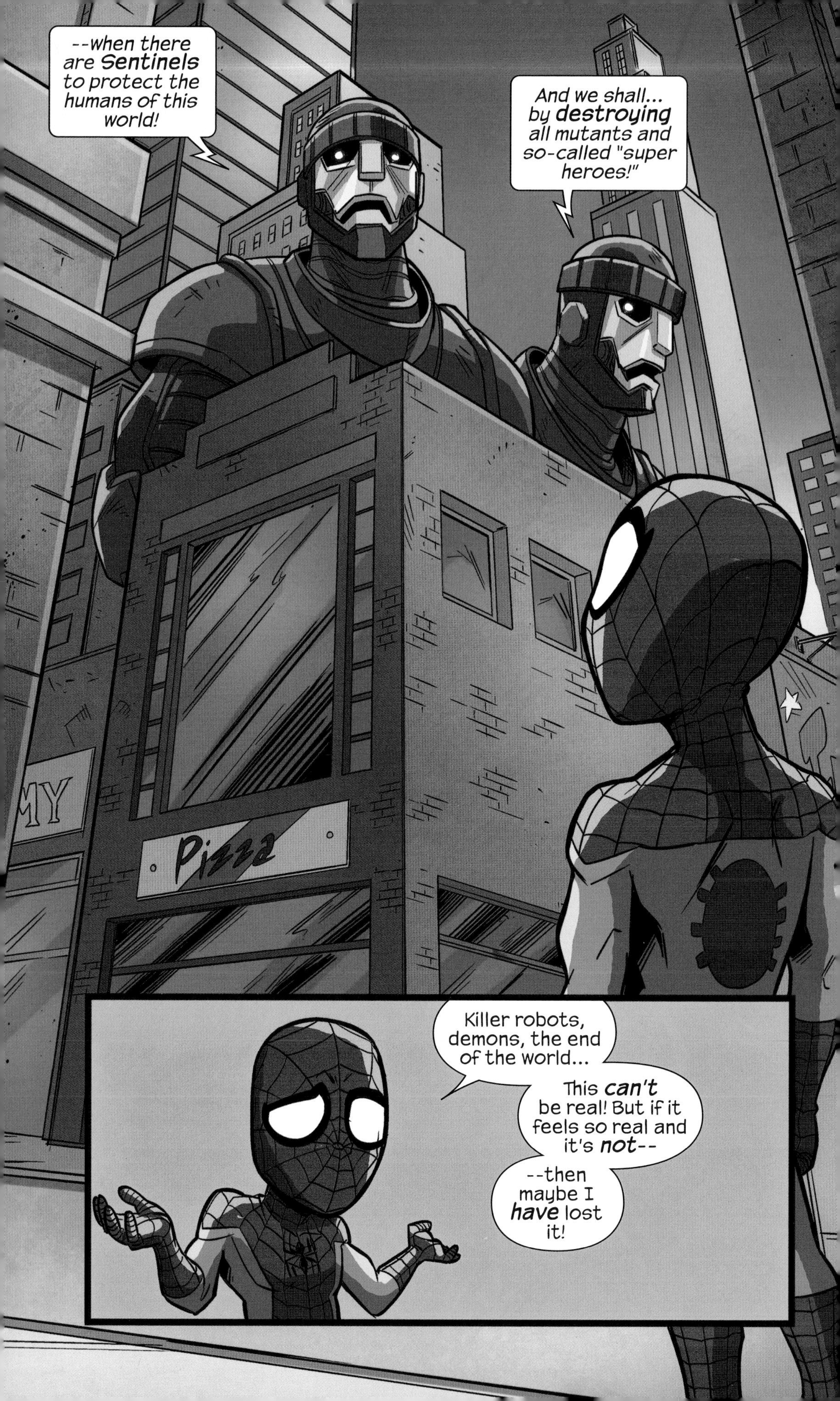

--when there are Sentinels to protect the humans of this world!
And we shall... by destroying all mutants and so-called "super heroes!"
MY
Pizza
Killer robots, demons, the end of the world...
This can't be real! But if it feels so real and it's not--
--then maybe I have lost it!

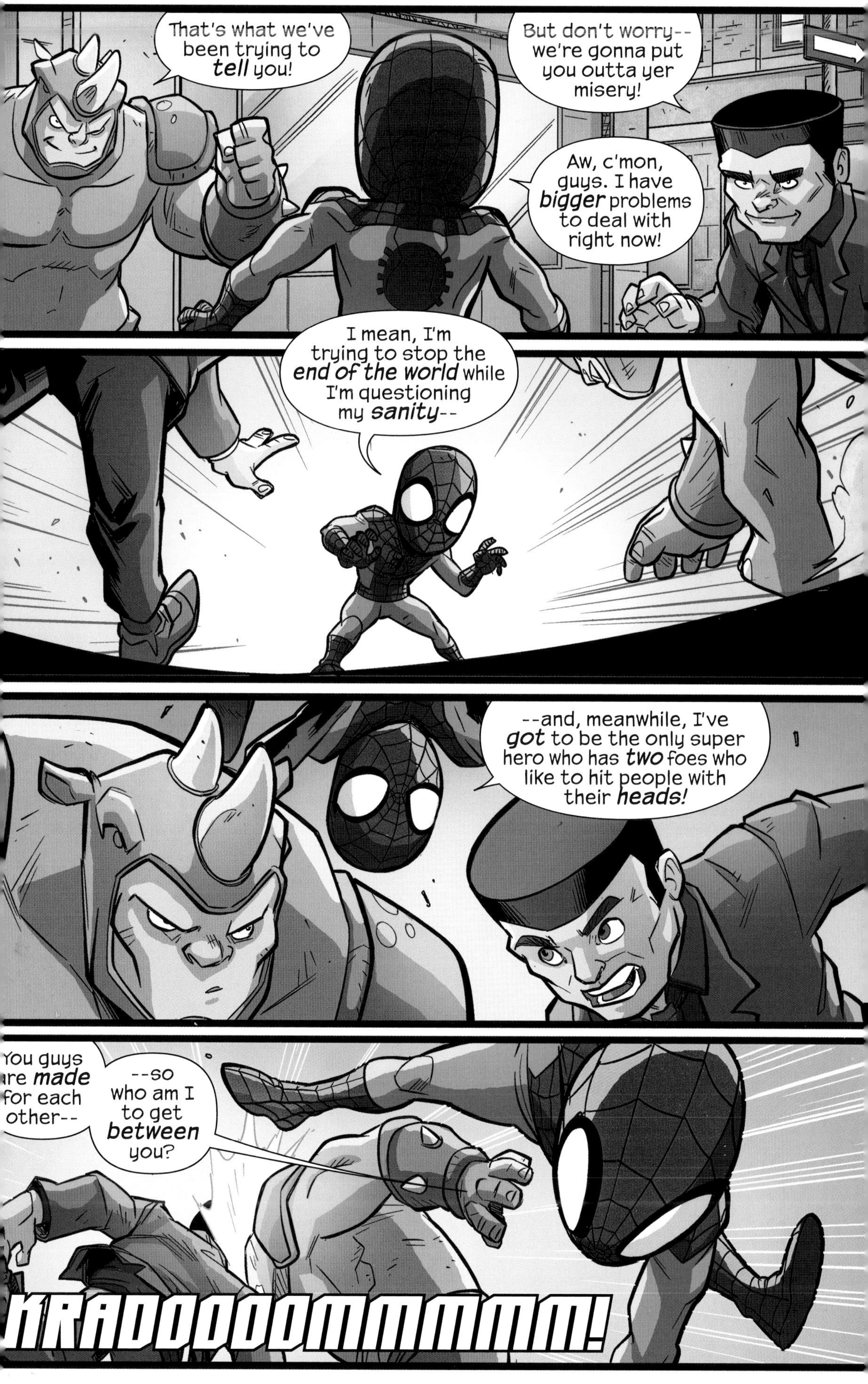
That's what we've been trying to *tell* you!
But don't worry-- we're gonna put you outta yer misery!
Aw, c'mon, guys. I have *bigger* problems to deal with right now!
I mean, I'm trying to stop the *end of the world* while I'm questioning my *sanity*--
--and, meanwhile, I've *got* to be the only super hero who has *two* foes who like to hit people with their *heads!*
You guys are *made* for each other--
--so who am I to get *between* you?
KRADOOOOMMMMMM!

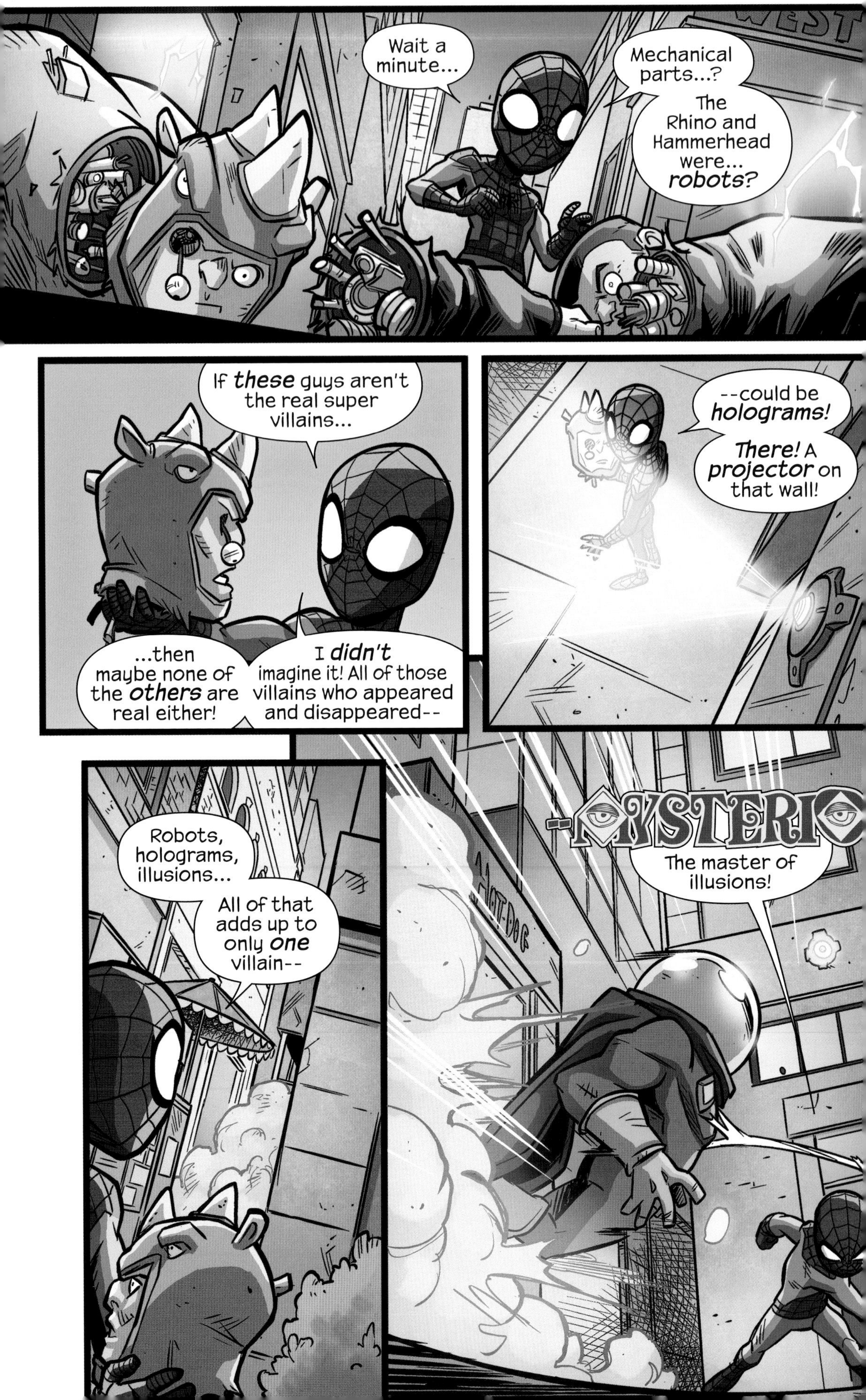

Wait a minute...
Mechanical parts...?
The Rhino and Hammerhead were... robots?
If these guys aren't the real super villains...
...then maybe none of the others are real either!
I didn't imagine it! All of those villains who appeared and disappeared--
--could be holograms!
There! A projector on that wall!
Robots, holograms, illusions...
All of that adds up to only one villain--
MYSTERIO
The master of illusions!

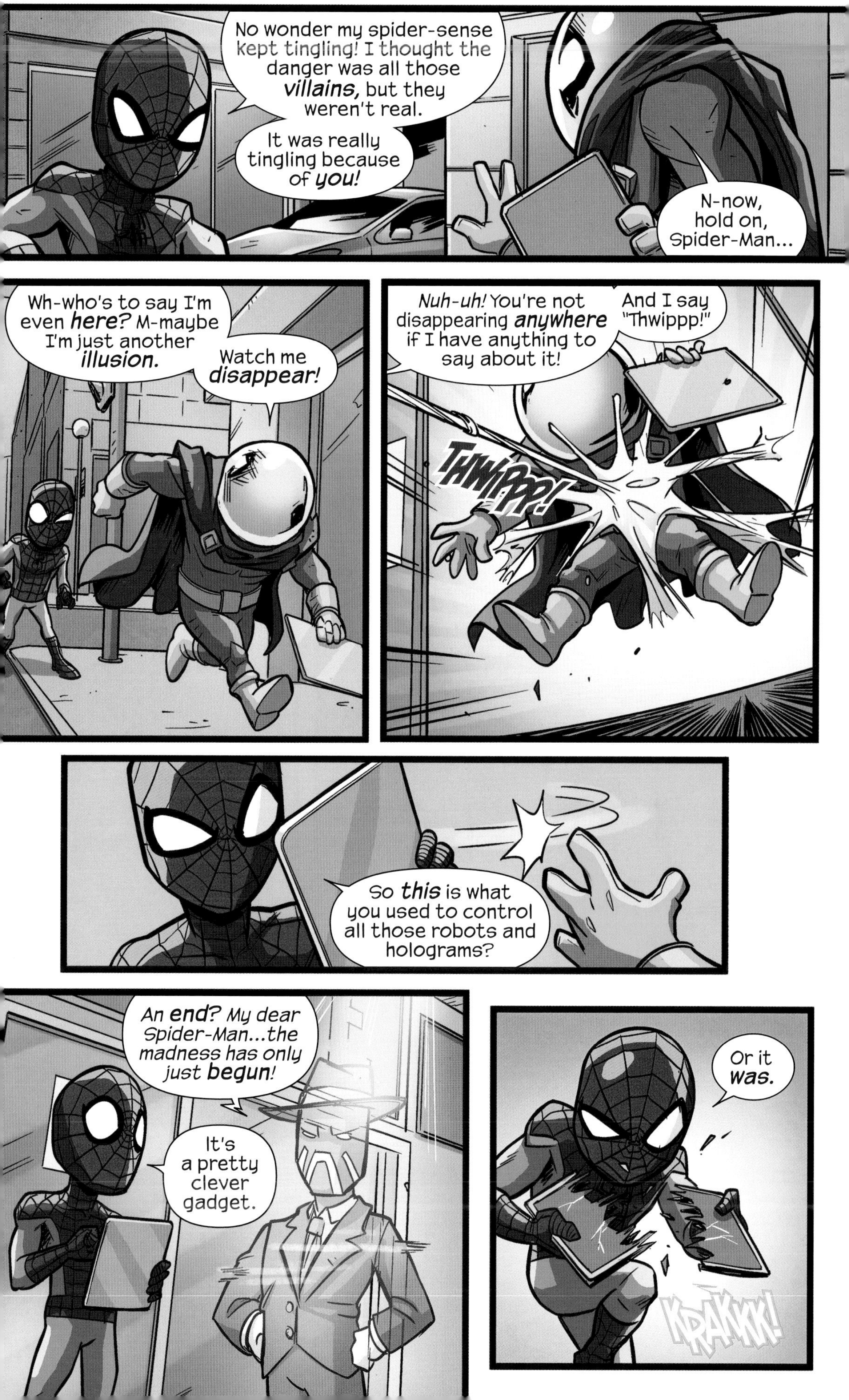
No wonder my spider-sense kept tingling! I thought the danger was all those *villains,* but they weren't real.
It was really tingling because of *you!*
N-now, hold on, Spider-Man...
Wh-who's to say I'm even *here?* M-maybe I'm just another *illusion.*
Watch me *disappear!*
Nuh-uh! You're not disappearing *anywhere* if I have anything to say about it!
And I say "Thwippp!"
THWIPPP!
So *this* is what you used to control all those robots and holograms?
It's a pretty clever gadget.
*An **end**? My dear Spider-Man...the madness has only just **begun**!*
Or it *was.*
KRAKKK!

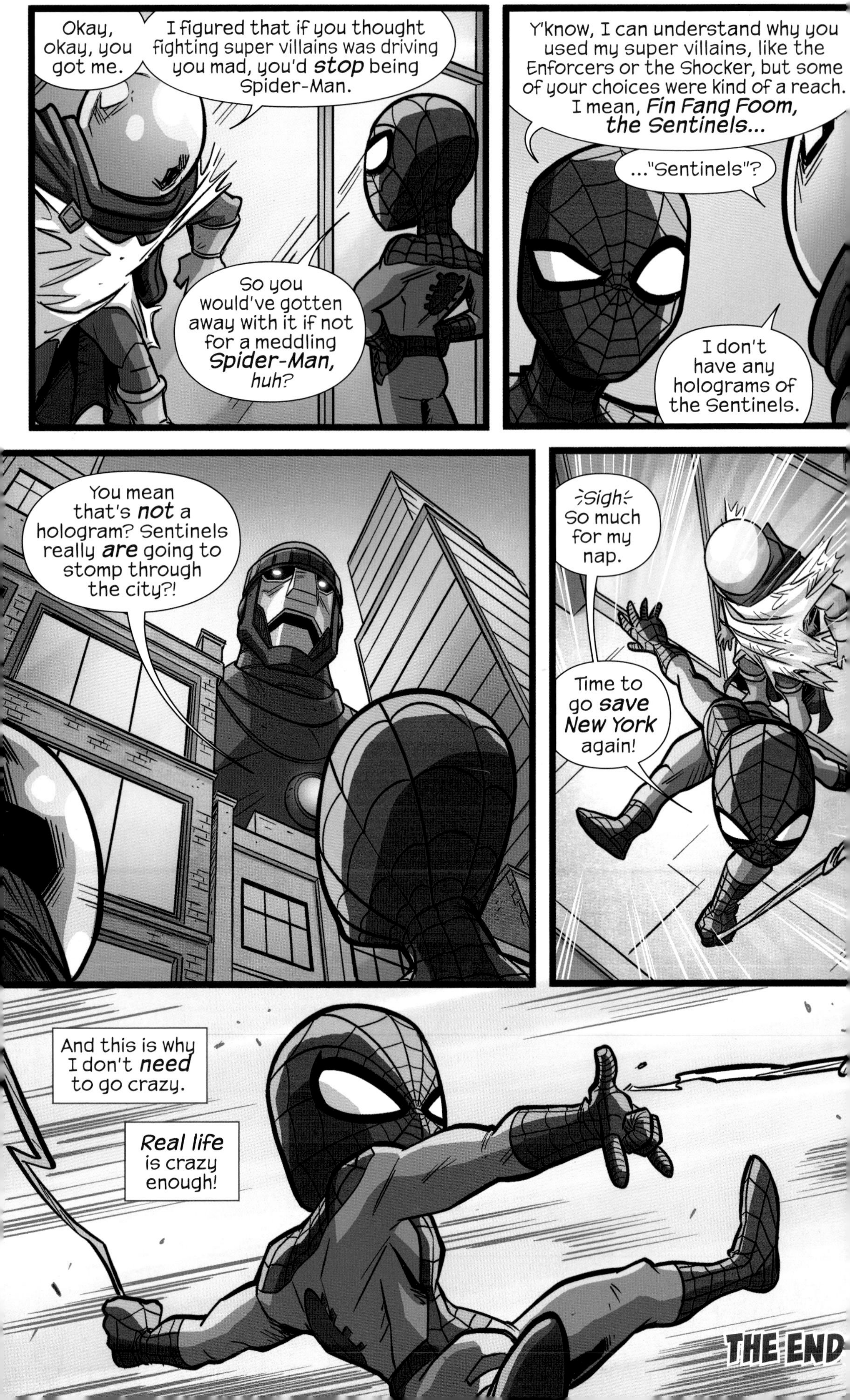
Okay, okay, you got me.
I figured that if you thought fighting super villains was driving you mad, you'd *stop* being Spider-Man.
So you would've gotten away with it if not for a meddling *Spider-Man,* huh?
Y'know, I can understand why you used my super villains, like the Enforcers or the Shocker, but some of your choices were kind of a reach. I mean, *Fin Fang Foom, the Sentinels...*
..."Sentinels"?
I don't have any holograms of the Sentinels.
You mean that's *not* a hologram? Sentinels really *are* going to stomp through the city?!
Sigh So much for my nap.
Time to go *save New York* again!
And this is why I don't *need* to go crazy.
Real life is crazy enough!
THE END

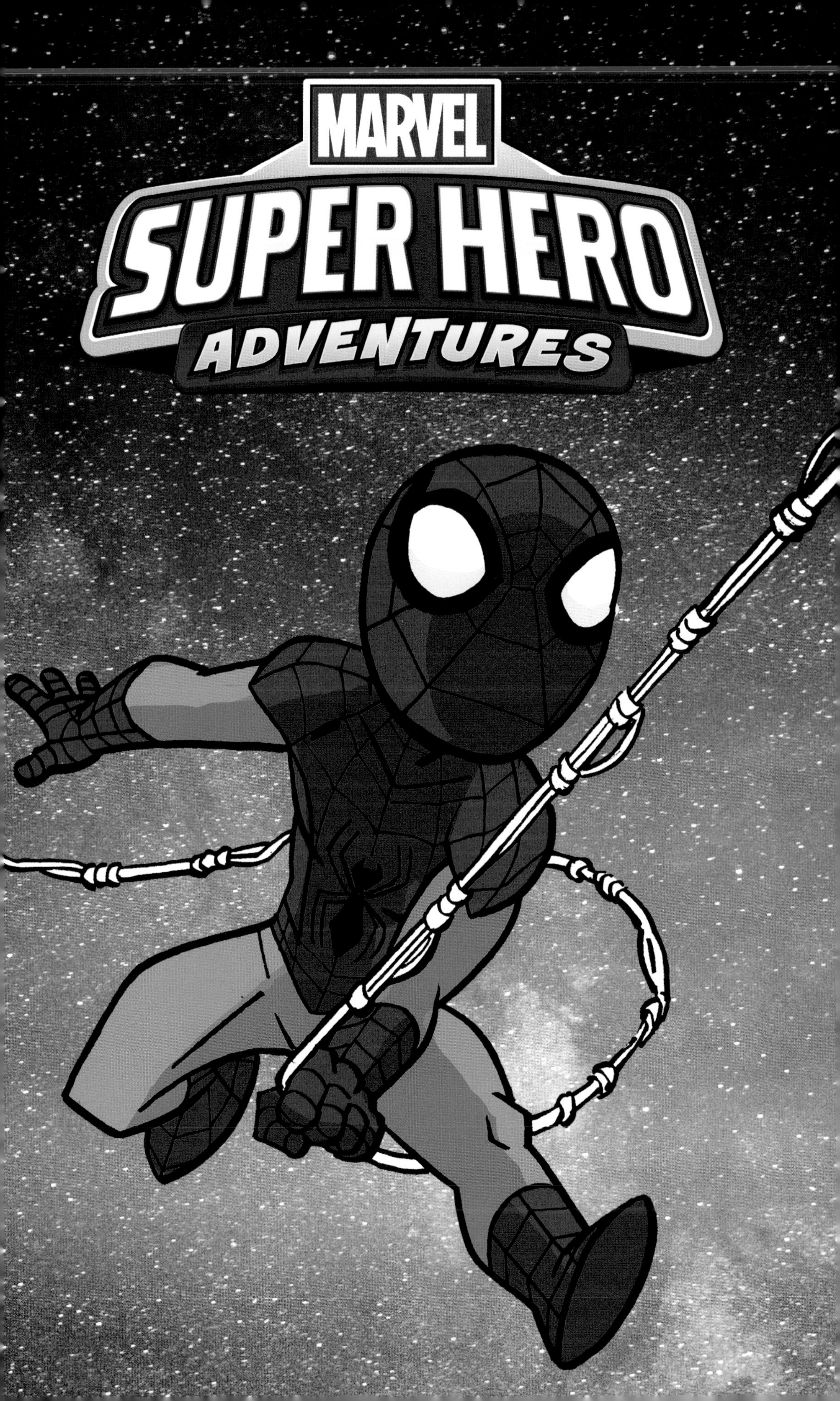
MARVEL
SUPER HERO
ADVENTURES

MARVEL SUPER HERO ADVENTURES

COLLECT THEM ALL!

Set of 13 Hardcover Books ISBN: 978-1-5321-4444-8

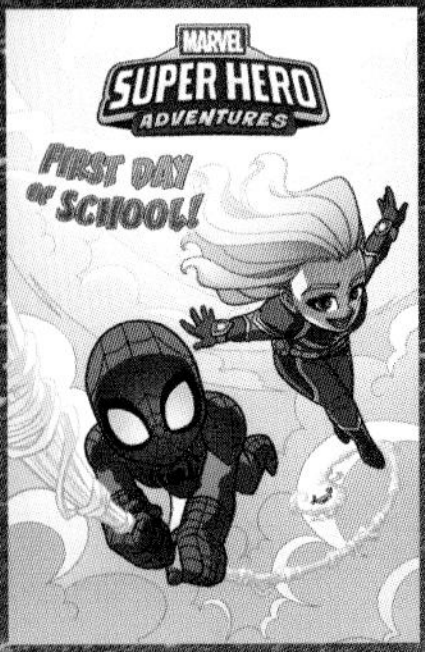
MARVEL SUPER HERO ADVENTURES
FIRST DAY OF SCHOOL!

Hardcover Book ISBN 978-1-5321-4445-5

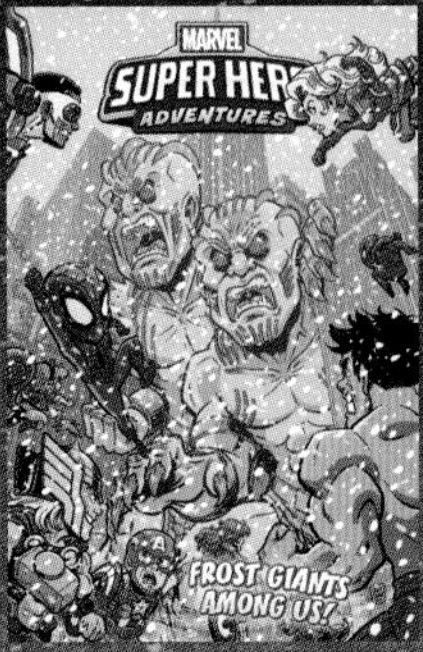
MARVEL SUPER HERO ADVENTURES
FROST GIANTS AMONG US!

Hardcover Book ISBN 978-1-5321-4446-2

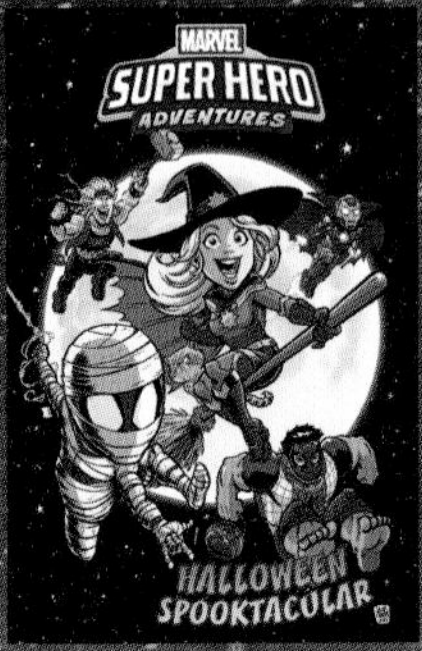
MARVEL SUPER HERO ADVENTURES
HALLOWEEN SPOOKTACULAR

Hardcover Book ISBN 978-1-5321-4447-9

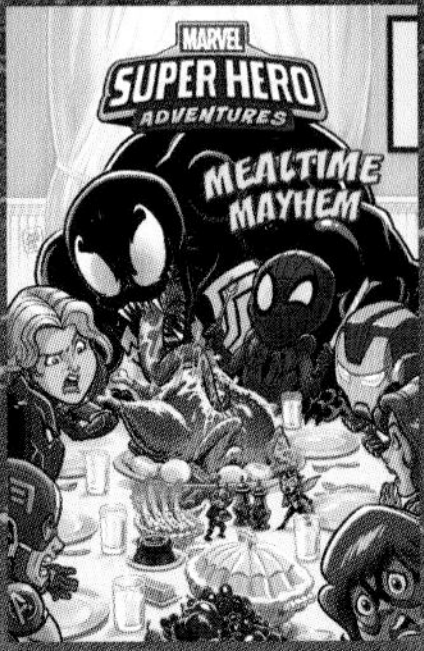
MARVEL SUPER HERO ADVENTURES
MEALTIME MAYHEM

Hardcover Book ISBN 978-1-5321-4448-6

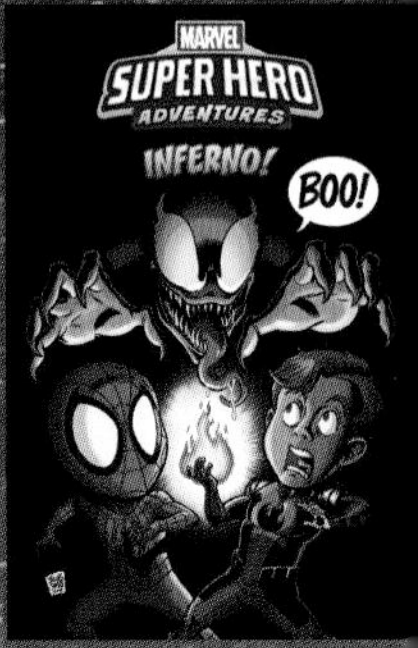
MARVEL SUPER HERO ADVENTURES
INFERNO!
BOO!

Hardcover Book ISBN 978-1-5321-4449-3

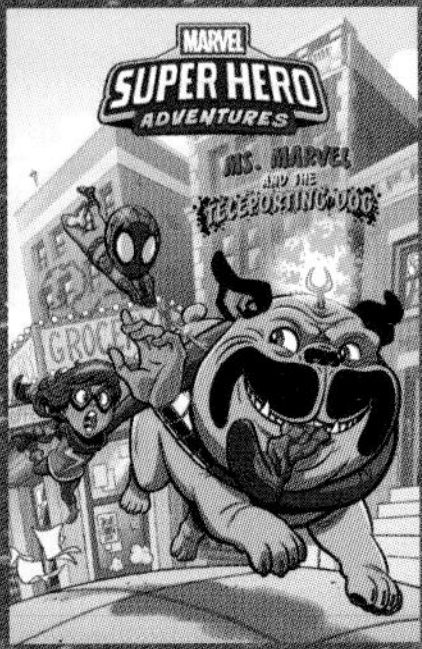
MARVEL SUPER HERO ADVENTURES
MS. MARVEL AND THE TELEPORTING DOG

Hardcover Book ISBN 978-1-5321-4450-9

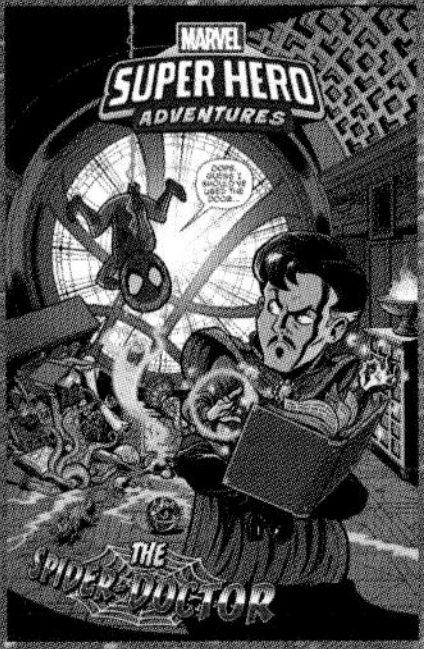
MARVEL SUPER HERO ADVENTURES
THE SPIDER-DOCTOR

Hardcover Book ISBN 978-1-5321-4451-6

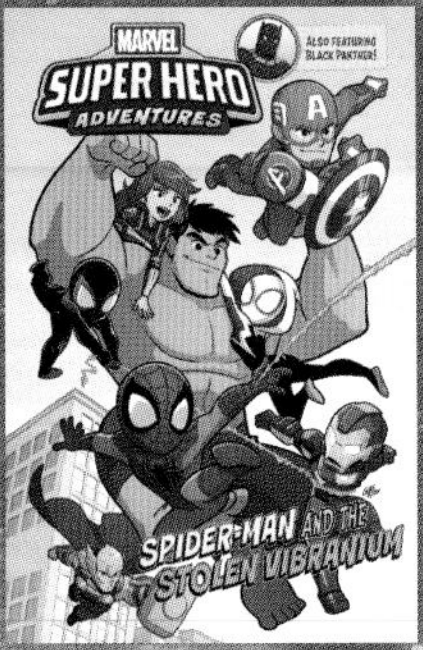
MARVEL SUPER HERO ADVENTURES
ALSO FEATURING BLACK PANTHER!
SPIDER-MAN AND THE STOLEN VIBRANIUM

Hardcover Book ISBN 978-1-5321-4452-3

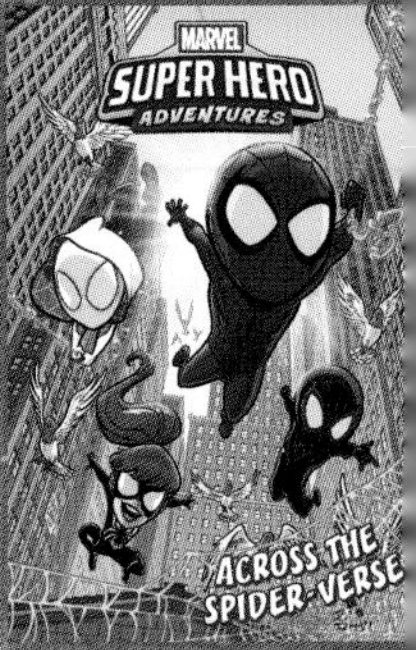
MARVEL SUPER HERO ADVENTURES
ACROSS THE SPIDER-VERSE

Hardcover Book ISBN 978-1-5321-4453-0

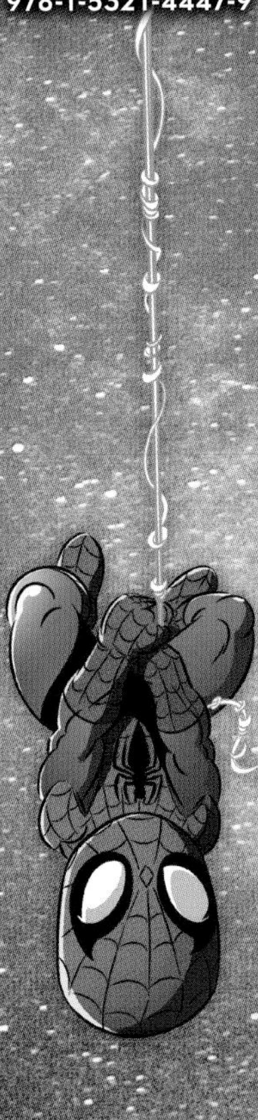

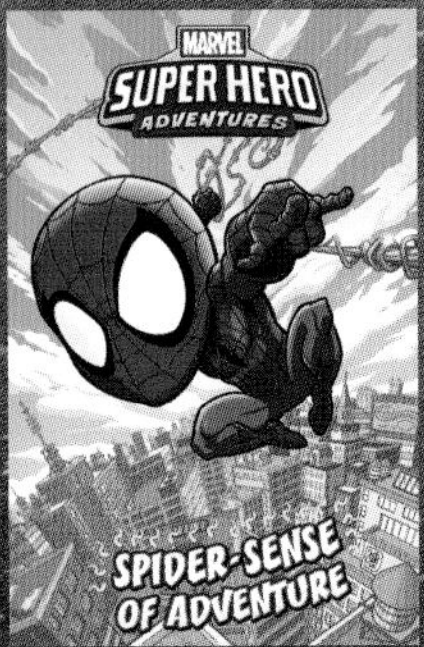
MARVEL SUPER HERO ADVENTURES
SPIDER-SENSE OF ADVENTURE

Hardcover Book ISBN 978-1-5321-4454-7

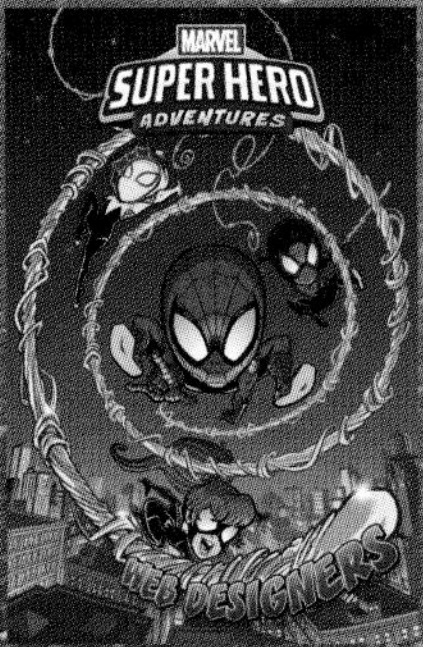
MARVEL SUPER HERO ADVENTURES
WEB DESIGNERS

Hardcover Book ISBN 978-1-5321-4455-4

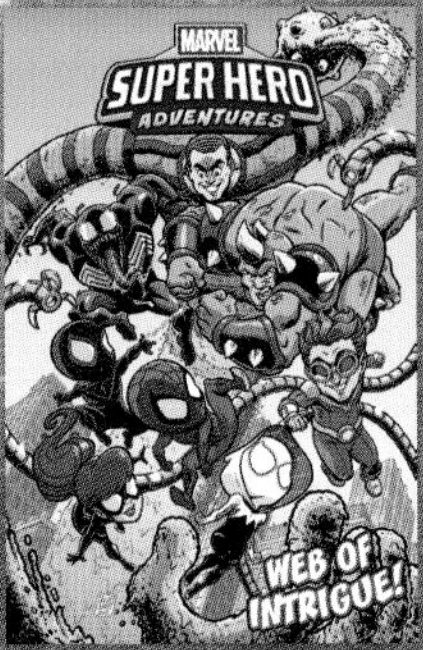
MARVEL SUPER HERO ADVENTURES
WEB OF INTRIGUE!

Hardcover Book ISBN 978-1-5321-4456-1

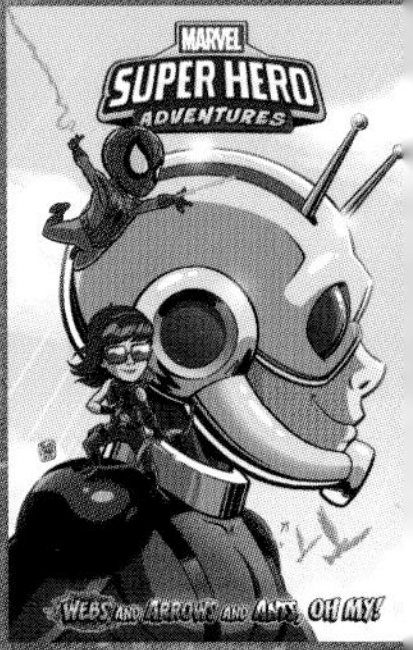
MARVEL SUPER HERO ADVENTURES
WEBS AND ARROWS AND ANTS, OH MY!

Hardcover Book ISBN 978-1-5321-4457-8